On Two Wheels

John Allan

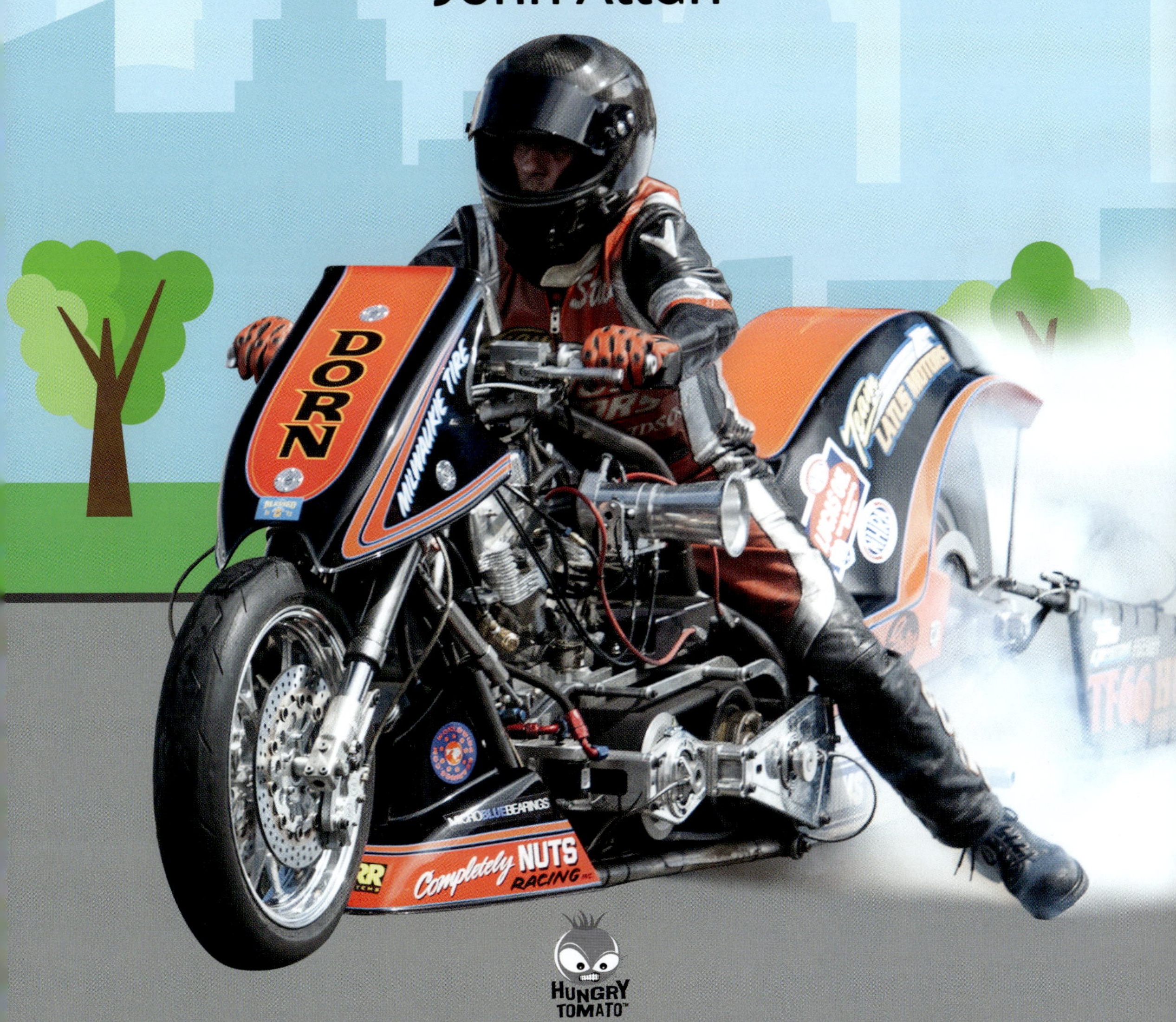

HUNGRY TOMATO™

First published in Great Britain in 2021 by
Hungry Tomato Ltd
F1, Old Bakery Studios
Blewetts Wharf
Malpas Road, Truro
Cornwall, TR1 1QH, UK

A CIP catalog record for this book is available from the British Library

ISBN 9781 913440 63 3

Manufactured in the USA

Discover more at
www.hungrytomato.com

Contents

Words that appear in **bold** are explained in the glossary

The Mighty Mechanics

We are the **Mighty Mechanics.** Welcome to our **workshop**. We work on some amazing vehicles, and here are a few of the **tools** we use to fix them.

Dodge Tomahawk

This motorcycle was built to reach speeds of 420mph (676 km/h), but nobody has tried to go that fast. At such a high speed, riders could easily be blown away!

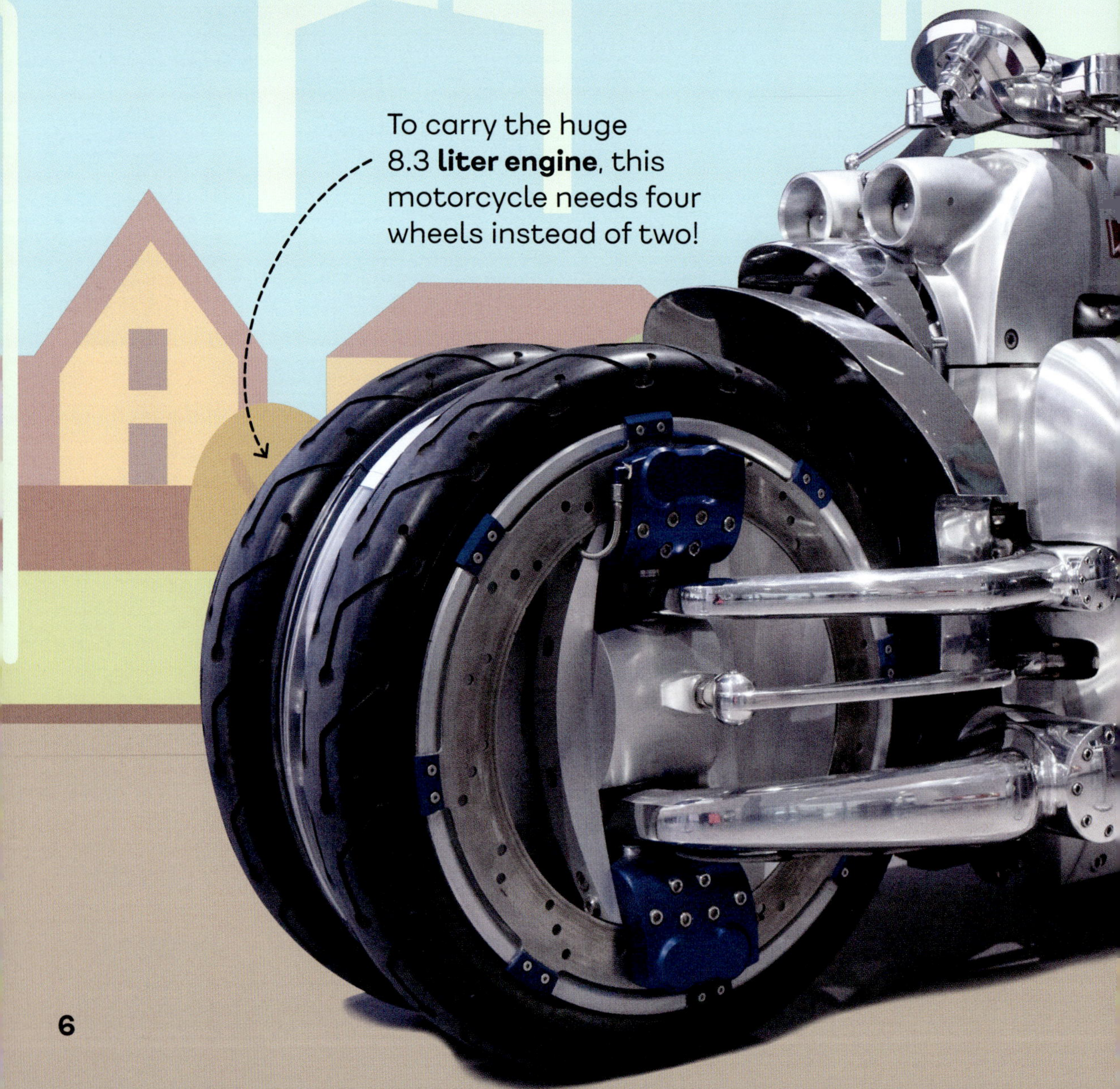

To carry the huge 8.3 **liter engine**, this motorcycle needs four wheels instead of two!

Each wheel can turn in different directions, so that it can lean into bends.

Only 9 of these superbikes were ever built. Each one cost $550,000!

Suzuki Hayabusa

This is the fastest motorcycle that can be ridden on ordinary roads. It can reach speeds of over 200 mph (322 km/h) and is named after the fastest animal on Earth.

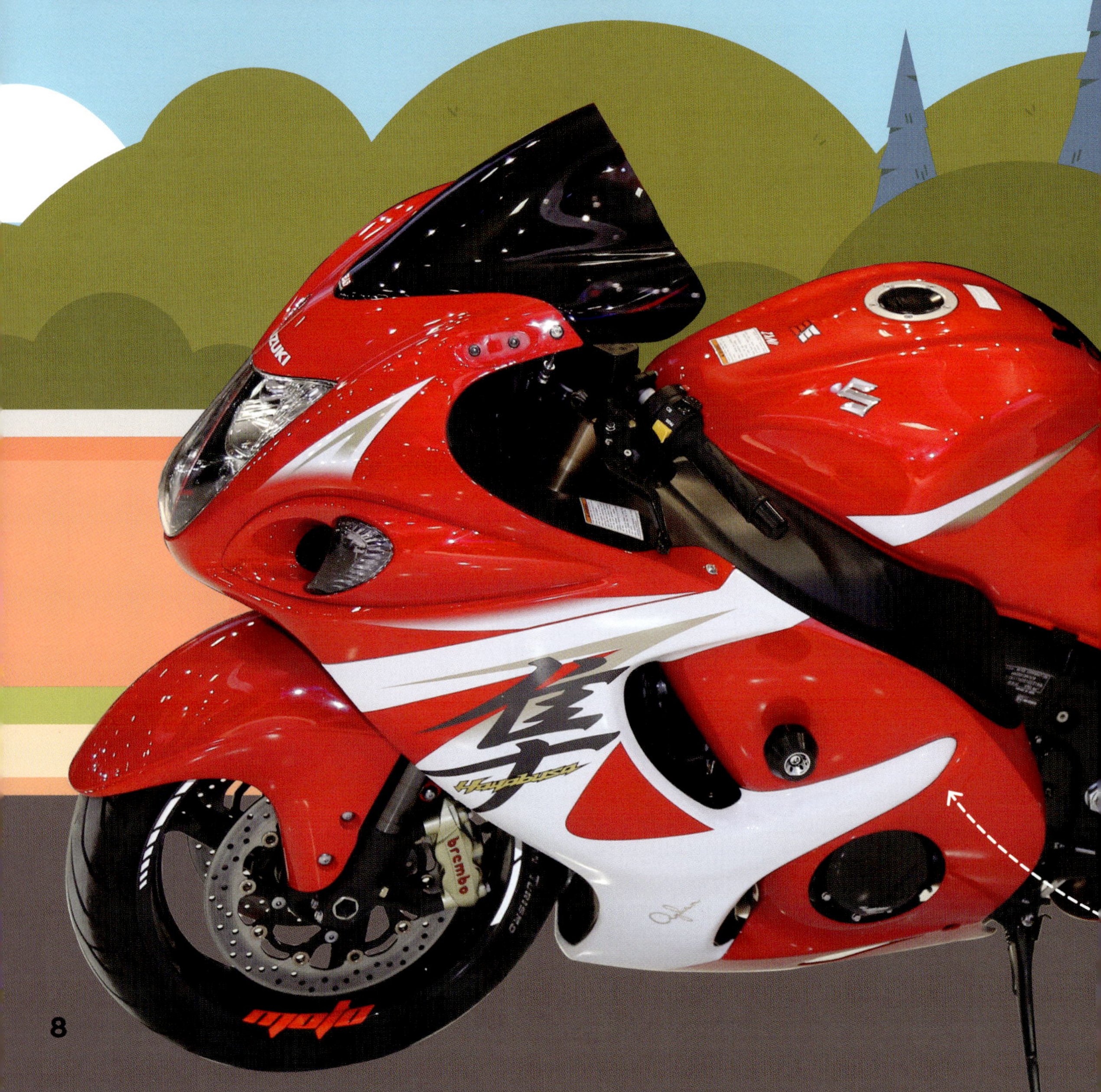

Hayabusa is Japanese for peregrine falcon.

These falcons can dive to attack prey at speeds of over 200 mph (322 km/h).

Its engine is so powerful, it has been used to power an airplane.

MotoGP

The fastest races on two wheels are **MotoGP**. This is short for **'Motorcycle Grand Prix'.** The riders can reach speeds of 221 mph (356 km/h).

The motorcycles lean over so far when traveling round corners that the rider's knees and elbows can scrape along the ground.

The rider's suit has an **airbag** that inflates, to protect the rider if they crash.

GP motorcycles can reach speeds of 200 mph (322 km/h) in less than 7 seconds.

Drag Racing on Two Wheels

Drag races take place on a short, straight course. Top drag motorcycles can reach speeds of 200 mph (322 km/h) in 660 feet (200 metres).

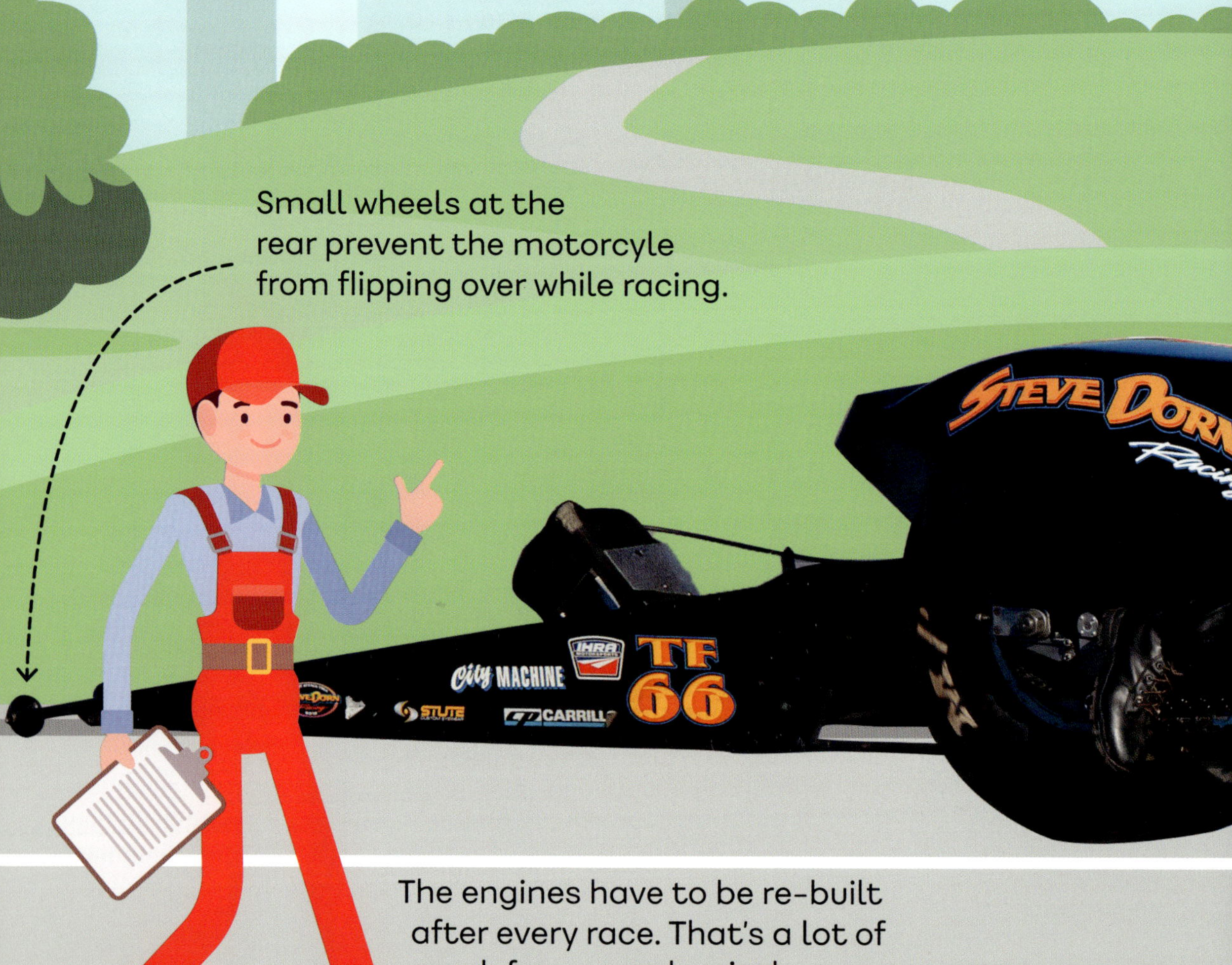

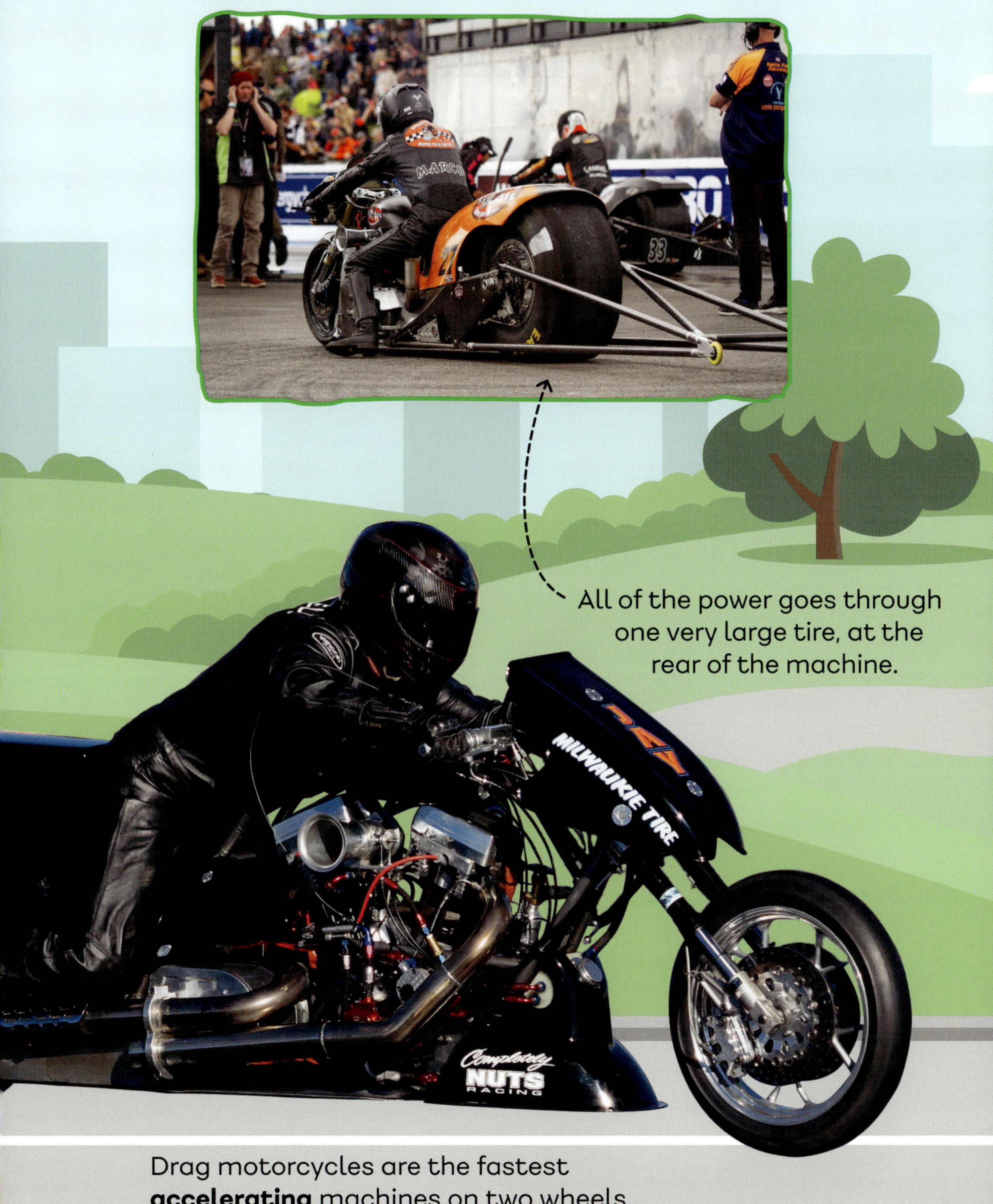

All of the power goes through one very large tire, at the rear of the machine.

Drag motorcycles are the fastest **accelerating** machines on two wheels.

Kawasaki Ninja H2R

The **H2R** is designed to be a racing motorcycle. It has reached a top speed of 248mph and costs a cool $40,000.

The bike needs to be checked and serviced after just 15 hours of use, which keeps us mechanics very busy.

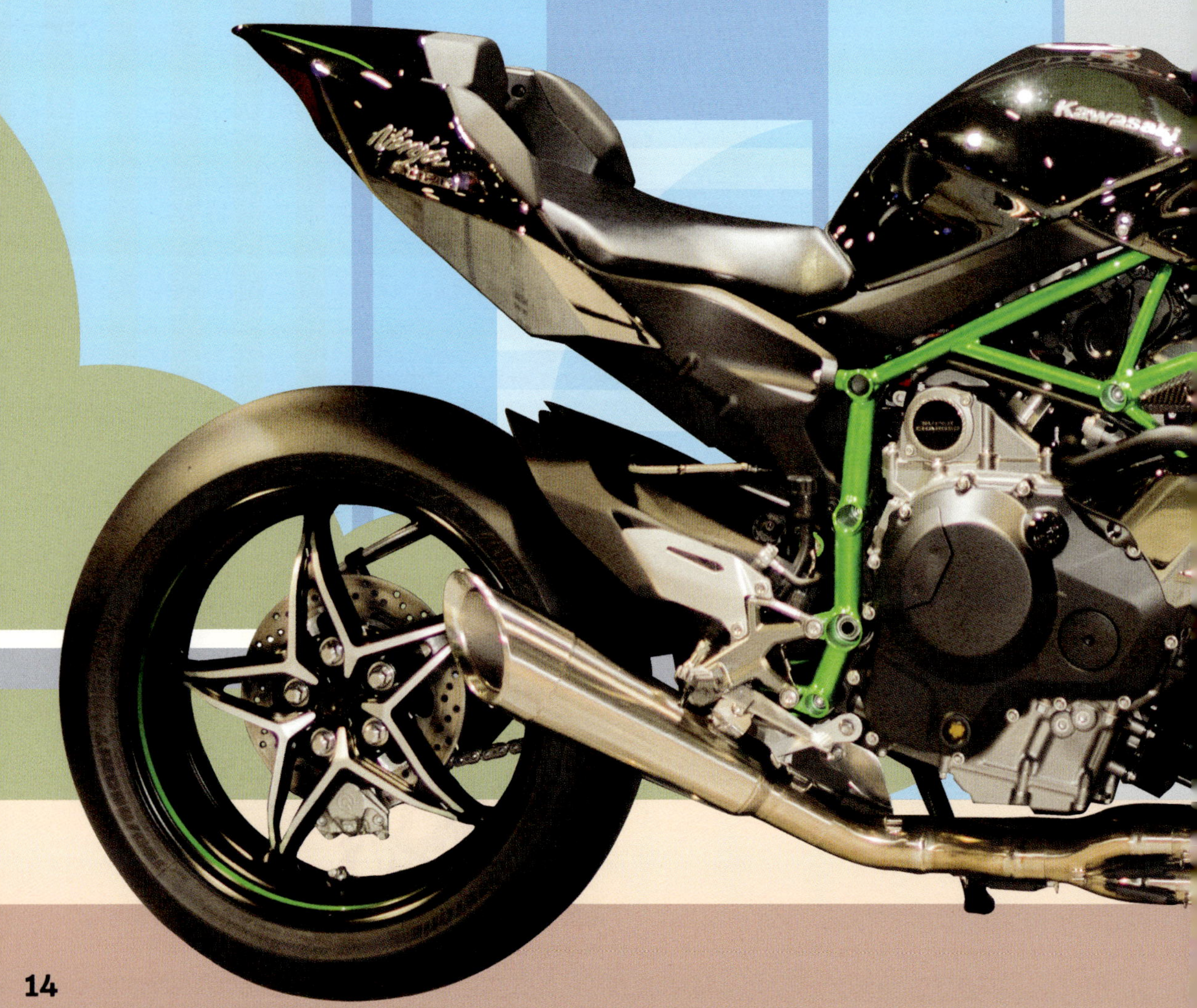

Controls can tell the rider how far they have leaned over, riding round bends.

This Kawasaki is named after Japanese **Ninja** warriors.

Harley-Davidson

Harley-Davidsons are not the fastest motorcycles, but they are probably one of the coolest. This is the **Forty-eight Speedster,** with a top speed of only 110 mph (177 km/h).

A Harley-Davidson was the first motorcycle to average over 100mph (161 km/h), at a 300 mile (483 kilometre) race in 1913.

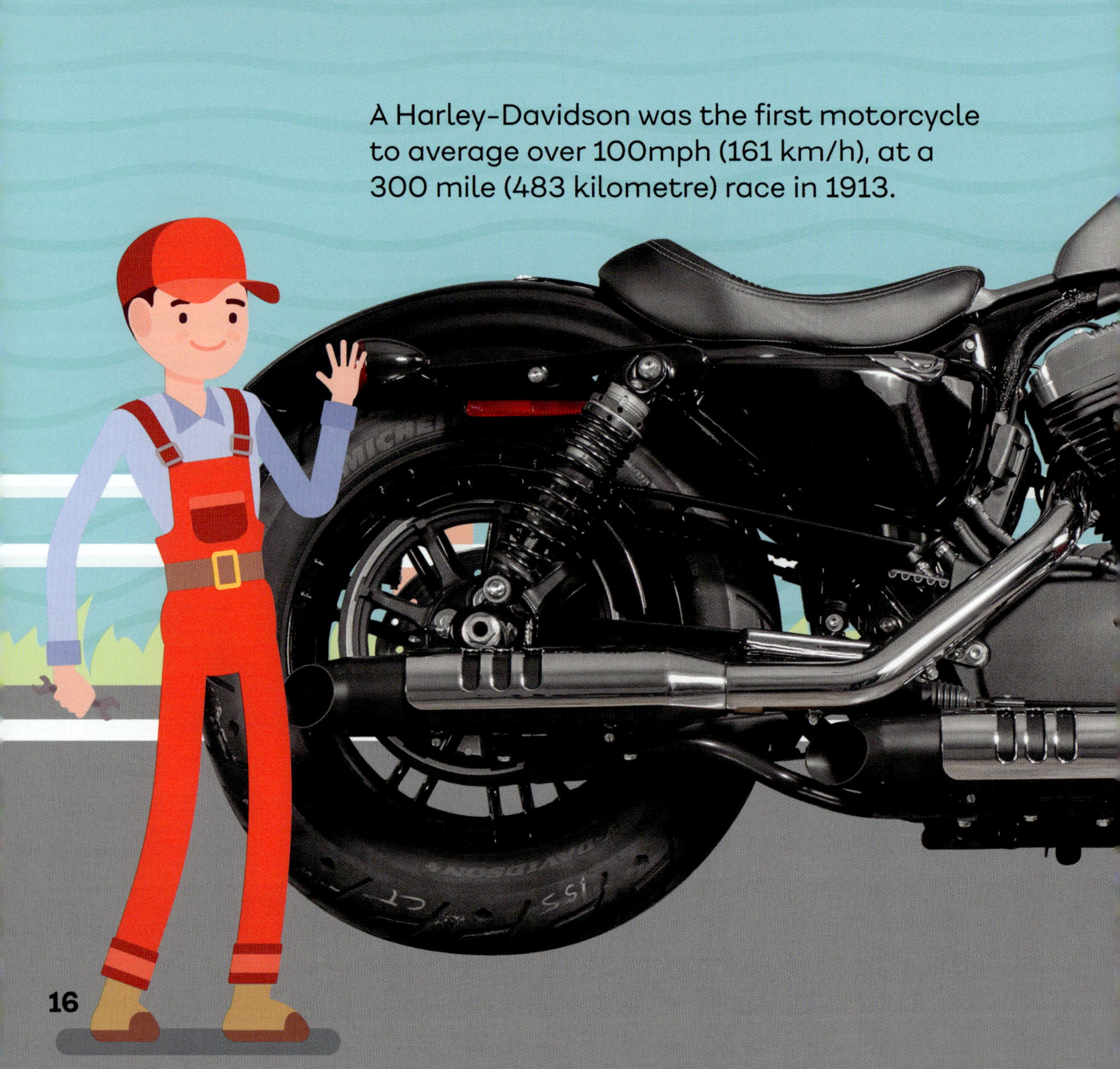

Harley-Davidson are famous for using a lot of **chrome** on their motorcycles.

Harleys are very comfortable, and great for long distance travel.

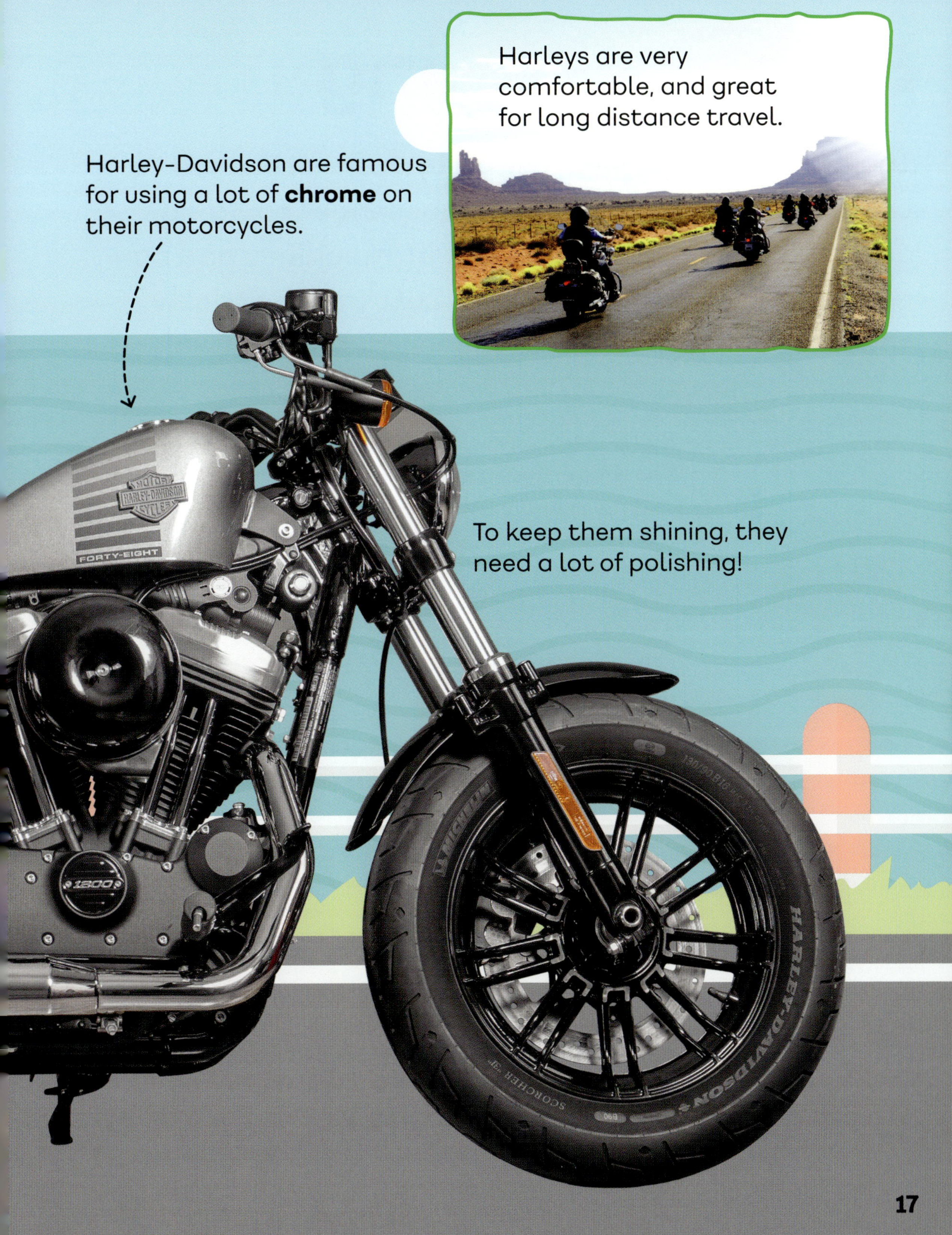

To keep them shining, they need a lot of polishing!

Sidecar Racing

The first **sidecar** was just a platform attached to the side of a motorcycle, so a passenger could ride along. Now, they are custom built machines and can reach speeds of over 160 mph (260 km/h). Strictly speaking, they have three wheels, instead of two!

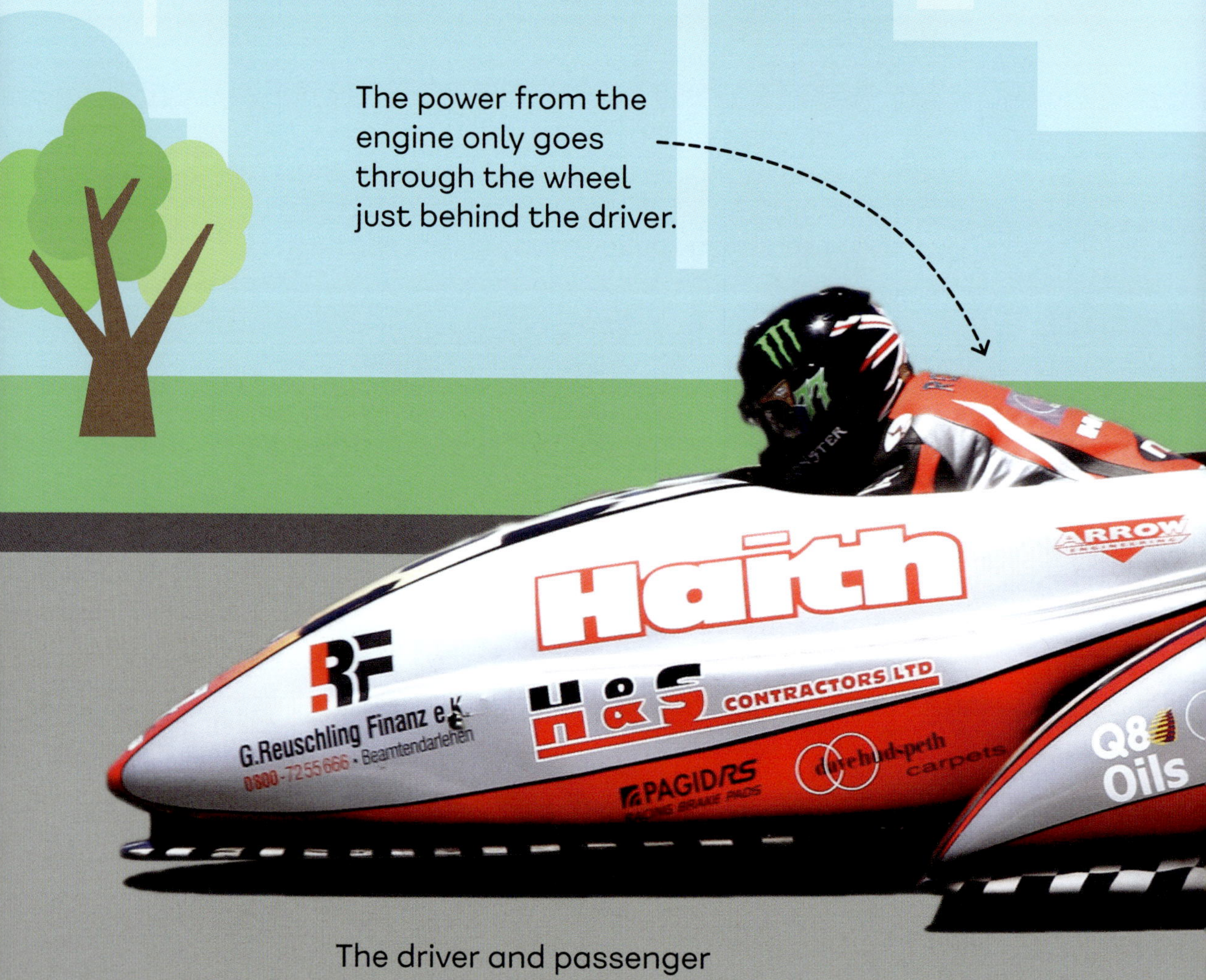

The power from the engine only goes through the wheel just behind the driver.

The driver and passenger have to work as a team.

This is Sidecarcross racing, which takes place on a motocross track.

The passenger moves around the vehicle and uses their weight to help the sidecar go faster around corners.

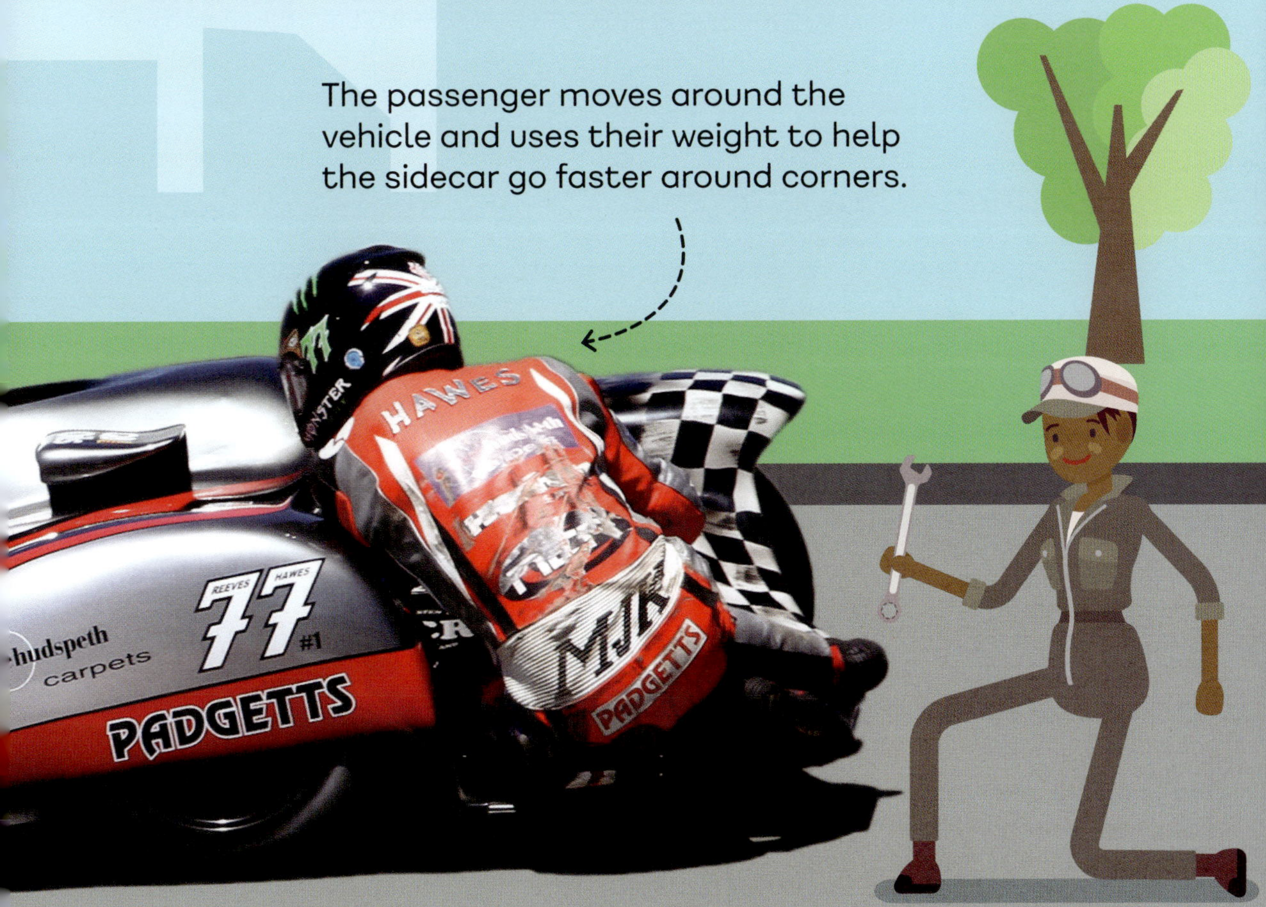

Road Racing Bicycles

Professional cyclists reach an average top speed of nearly 30 mph (48km/h). They're not as fast as a top motorcycle – but they power the cycles themselves.

This is the Tour de France, where 176 riders race over 2,200 miles (3,500 kilometres) in 21 days.

A top racing bike costs over $12,000 and weighs only 18 pounds (8 kilograms).

The record for the fastest person on a bicycle is 167 mph (268 km/h) and was set by Fred Rompelberg, cycling in the **slipstream** of a truck.

Flat Track Racing

Flat track racing is competed on oval tracks, where the riders can reach speeds of 140 mph (225 km/h) on the straights and 90 mph (145 km/h) around the corners.

The riders use their feet to help the motorcycle slide round the corners.

These motorcycles have one brake on the rear wheel, but it's hardly ever used.

After every race the mechanics have to take each motorcycle apart and re-build it.

Men and women compete side by side in this sport.

Glossary

accelerating increasing speed.

airbag a bag of air that is designed to inflate very quickly to protect the rider in a crash.

chrome is a decorative and protective metal coating.

liter engines the size of an engine is measured by how many liters of liquid it can hold.

ninja is a Japanese warrior skilled in moving very quietly without being seen.

slipstream is when a rider follows another rider or object that stops the air from slowing them down.

superbike refers to a motorcycle with a large engine.

Measuring Speed

A vehicle's speed is usually measured in either **miles per hour (mph)** or **kilometers per hour (km/h).**

1 mph = 1.6 km/h

Picture Credits

(abbreviations: t = top; b = bottom; m = middle; l = left; r = right; bg = background)

Shutterstock: Abdul Razak Latif 11tr; Amanita Silvicora 10bg; Anatoliy Lukich 22m; Andrew Rybalko (mechanics illustrations); AndrisRphoto 19tl; Archiwiz 4l; Betto Rodrigues 14m; cate_89 17tr; Dan Moeller 2m, 20m; DniproDD 1bg, 18bg, 24bg; Eugene Onischenko 23m; EvrenKalinbacak 8m; KPG Payless2 15tr; Harry Collins Photography 9tr; Ivan Garcia 10m; Joshua Rainey Photography 12m; Julia Lazebnaya 12bg; KitiphongPho30 16m; Lario Tus 18m; Mastak A 2bg, 16bg; MicroOne 6bg; Mikhail Martynov 5b; Nigel Buckner 13tr; Oleksandr Derevianko 22bg; ProStockStudio 20bg; ProStockStudio 8bg; robuarts 14bg; Sergii Rudiuk 21t; SunflowerMomma 6m; Vectorpocket 4bg; Volodymyr Krasyuk 4mb, 5mr.